Tymple's Tantrum

Written by Tymple Reign
Illustrated by Aria Jones

Copyright©

Written by Tymple Reign &
Illustrated by Aria Jones
ISBN: 978-0-578-86418-1 (hardcover)
ISBN: 978-1-7923-6220-0 (paperback)
ISBN: 978-1-7923-6219-4 (ebook)
Printed in the United States of America
First printing edition in February 2021

Author's Acknowledgements

Thanks to Mommy for always being here and helping me get my book out. Thanks to Daddy for telling me not to be afraid to express myself. My voice is being heard. Thanks to Grandma for always letting me choose my special toys. Thanks to Theory, my best friend, Belly Buddy, and inspiration. I love you all.

Dedication

This book is dedicated to my Grandy. We miss and love you. Continue to watch over us.

Hello, I am Tymple. I am seven years old.

I have a twin brother. His name is Theory. He is my best friend sometimes. Sometimes he is not my best friend though. Today he is not because he played with my toys when I didn't want him to. He doesn't let me have a turn when he is playing the X-Box and makes me wait forever.

He splashes water on me when we are in the swimming pool and he knows I don't like water in my face.

3

But today I am mad for a different reason. I am really mad because I cannot go outside to ride my scooter. Mommy said that we must do our homework first. I do not want to do my homework first! I want to ride my scooter first! So I will get mad and then Mommy will let me ride my scooter.

4

I will poke my lip out! I will stomp my feet! I will cross my arms and let the whole family know that I am mad!

Mommy walks in the kitchen and sees me with my lip poked out. But she doesn't say anything.

Daddy walks in the living room and sees me with my lip poked out. Now, I'm stomping my feet. But he doesn't say anything.

Theory sees me walk into his room with my lip poked out, stomping my feet, and crossing my arms. He doesn't say anything either! Now I am really angry! "I am so maaaaad!" I screamed.

I started crying really loud. "Tymple, what is wrong?" asked Mommy. "Why are you crying?" She looked worried as she walked closer to me. "Mommy, I am mad because you won't let me ride my scooter," I said sobbing.

9

"Tymple, we have rules in this family and in life, for a reason," Mommy made clear. "You have to learn to follow the rules. Mommy and Daddy are adults and we have rules. Just because you get mad doesn't mean you can have your way. The older you get, you will learn more about responsibility. Doing your homework is a responsible thing to do."

10

"I want you to have fun, but you have to do your homework first. Homework helps you learn and get good grades. Throwing a temper tantrum is not being a big girl because it is not a responsible thing to do," Mommy explained.

11

"What is a Tymple tantrum Mommy?" I asked. "That's funny because you are Tymple throwing a tantrum, but not a T-y-m-p-l-e tantrum, but a t-e-m-p-e-r tantrum.

A temper tantrum is when you are angry and your actions show that you are angry. People have tantrums when they lose control

13

Now what if Mommy had a temper tantrum because I have to do things? Daddy wouldn't like it if I have a temper tantrum because I don't want to cook. Theory wouldn't like it if I have a temper tantrum because I don't want to help him fly his drone.

You wouldn't like it if I have a temper tantrum
because I don't want to take you shopping to buy your
favorite things, now would you?

What if I poked out my lip, stomped my feet, and crossed my arms when I got mad because I have to follow the rules?" she questioned.

16

I guess Mommy did notice I was doing those things after all. I looked at Mommy puzzled because I am a BIG GIRL and I don't want to look like I lose control. I decided to do the responsible thing. I went to my desk and started my homework. It did not take me long at all to finish. Mommy checked my answers to make sure they were right. "Now that you are finished with your homework, Tymple, you may go outside and ride your scooter," Mommy explained with a smile.

I was so happy. I ran to the garage and put on my helmet, my elbow pads, and my knee pads. Wearing a helmet and being safe is also a responsible thing to do.

18

Theory was still doing his homework. I noticed that his lip was poked out.

He stood up, stomped his feet, and crossed his arms. I told him, "it's okay! Don't have a tantrum. Finish your homework and you can come outside and ride with me. It's the responsible thing to do, Theory!" He put his lip back in, stopped stomping his feet, uncrossed his arms, and sat back down at his desk.

After he finished his homework, Theory came outside too. We had fun racing each other down the street.

21

Mommy and Daddy came outside and talked to the neighbors. Our parents liked watching us race on our scooters.

Mommy almost fell because her shoestring came untied. I told her to tie her shoe because that was not being a "big girl" and it is not a responsible thing to do. We all laughed.

We rode our scooters until it was dinner time.

The End

About the Author

Tymple Reign is a young author, who made her writing debut at only 7 years old. Staying at home during the Covid-19 Pandemic, Tymple Reign thought it would be a good idea to start writing books so that she and her brother "wouldn't be bored." She wrote "Tymple's Tantrum" as she reflected on her attitude from not being able to attend school due to Covid-19. As a second grader, she wants other kids her age to be able to read her fun story-telling books. This talented author writes the type of fun books that she likes to read herself. Tymple Reign loves modeling, traveling, listening to music, and spending time with family. With such a vivid imagination and her love of unicorns, bunnies, kittens, and butterflies, readers can expect many more books from this beautiful, young author.